NEIGHBORING
VILLAGE

DANCE FIELD

THE PUMP

Miryam's Dance

By **Kerry Olitzky** and
Rachel Stock Spilker

Illustrated by
John Baptist Tumuhaise

APPLES & HONEY PRESS

To honor the memory of Jerome Reznick, z"l, for whom I am named. —KO

For the real Gilah, who is an inspiration. —RSS

To my loving wife and son, who have been a huge support in creating this book. —JBT

Apples & Honey Press • An imprint of Behrman House
Millburn, New Jersey 07041 • www.applesandhoneypress.com

ISBN 978-1-68115-608-8
Library of Congress Control Number: 2023937803

Edited by Aviva Lucas Gutnick
Design and Endpapers by Alexandra N. Segal
Printed in the United States of America

9 8 7 6 5 4 3 2 1

One Friday morning in a small village in Uganda, Miryam woke to the sound of a drumbeat. It was quiet and far away.

She peeked out the window and saw some guinea fowl scratching the dry ground. A gray-crowned crane greeted the day.

The distant drumbeat vibrated through her body. The sound made her want to dance.

"Listen to that wonderful sound," Miryam gushed.

"Come on, sleepyhead. You must still be dreaming," said Maama Wange. "Time for you to gather fruit and eggs and water. Shabbat is coming."

Outside their house, Miryam cartwheeled past her brothers sweeping the path.

"I just cleaned that and you're making a mess!" said Akiva.

"Do you hear the drumbeat?" Miryam asked.

"Of course I do," Akiva responded. "It's coming from the next village. But I also hear Taata Wange telling me to finish sweeping so everything is clean for Shabbat!"

Miryam pranced toward the mango and pawpaw trees.

"Ah, there you are! I've been waiting for you," said her friend Aliza. "We need to collect enough fruit to make our Shabbat sweet."

Miryam, barely listening, almost dropped the fruit. She was too busy straining to hear the drumbeat.

TOOMBA TOOMBA

"Do you hear it?"

Aliza sighed.

Miryam twirled to the store, already forgetting what Maama Wange wanted her to buy.

The shopkeeper, Mr. Okello, smiled. "Are you here for the plantains your mother needs to make matoke for Shabbat dinner?"

Miryam checked her list and nodded. She paid Mr. Okello and added the plantains to her sack.

SHOPPING LIST

Miryam skipped away,
heading toward her cousins in their yard.

"Your mother needs this to make challah,"
said one, handing her a large egg.
"Walk carefully with it. We can't enjoy
Shabbat without challah," another one said.

"Do you hear the drumbeat?" Miryam asked as she
pirouetted toward home, ignoring his advice.

On her way, Miryam smelled curry stew cooking in the village's outdoor kitchen.

She handed the fruit and egg to her mother.

"Where is the water?" Taata Wange asked.
Amid her excitement about the drumbeat,
Miryam had forgotten.

Her father sighed and
playfully tossed her
an empty jug.

"Catch," he said.
Miryam danced away
quickly toward the pump.

At the pump, Miryam filled
her jug. The drumbeat
was getting louder.

"Do you hear that?" she squealed
to no one in particular.

She whirled off
toward the sound.

Through the trees, Miryam saw a group of dancers
practicing in a field. They wore brightly colored
costumes with seed-filled shakers wrapped around
their ankles. Some had pots on their heads.

Drums of all sizes surrounded them.

Miryam watched the dancers move their hips in quick circles.

Fascinated, she held her hands up high and followed the movements.

Before she realized it, Miryam had danced her way into the open field.

One of the dancers spotted her and came over.

"I'm Gilah," she said.

"You are small and graceful like a kob antelope."

A tall boy handed her some pots.

"Here, try to balance these on your head.
Take your time and feel the rhythm."

Miryam stacked the pots on her head. She s-l-o-w-l-y stretched out her arms, feeling like she was on top of Mount Stanley.

As the drumbeat grew faster and louder, the other dancers circled her. Miryam carefully swayed to the *toomba toomba toom.*

The music slowed and then stopped.

"That was amazing," said Miryam, beaming.

Gilah handed Miryam the jug she'd left near the tree. "We are practicing for our Shabbat dance in Nabugoya tonight. Will you join us?"

Miryam squealed with joy.
"Yes! That's my village!"

Gilah hugged Miryam.
"See you soon."

Back in Nabugoya, the villagers were starting to gather around a large table already set with the Shabbat candles.

The rabbi brought banana wine and fresh grape juice.
Miryam's cousin carried the warm, fresh challah.
Miryam handed the water jug to her father.

Every week on Shabbat, the otherwise busy village slowed down.
Everyone could relax and enjoy being together with family and friends.

Suddenly, a drumbeat broke the stillness.

Dancers paraded toward the village center and formed a circle.

Gilah motioned for Miryam to join them.

Her parents frowned.

"Miryam, this is not the time for dancing.

We need to light the candles," said Maama Wange.

Miryam glanced at the dancers,
then back at her parents.
This was her chance.
"Please, Maama and Taata Wange.
This is also a way to celebrate Shabbat,"
she said. They paused and thought for a
moment. Then they smiled and nodded.

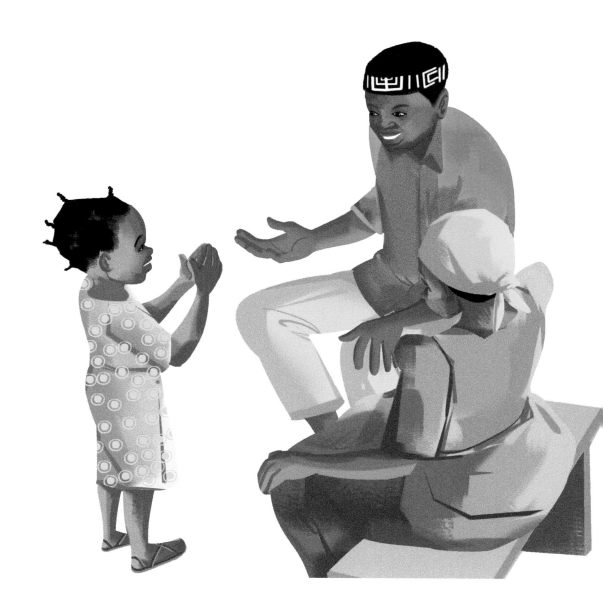

Miryam leaped up to join the dance troupe.
The villagers clapped along to the beat, slowly at first,
watching the dancers but unsure about this new Friday evening
experience. Then they too began to feel the rhythm and
whoop-whooped as the dancers spun and swayed. Maama
Wange smiled and Taata Wange tapped his feet.

Miryam spread her arms out wide,
lifted her head, and moved her entire
body to every *toomba toomba* of the drum.
She passed by Maama Wange and
stretched out a hand to her.

Maama Wange hesitated.
She looked around.

Then hand in hand, Miryam and her mother danced,
filled with Shabbat joy.

Welcome to Uganda!

**My name is Gershom Sizomu
and I am the chief rabbi of Uganda.**

You might be surprised to learn there are rabbis in my African country. In fact, my community has about two thousand people practicing Judaism. We are called the Abayudaya, which is a word for "People of Judah" in the Luganda language.

We live peacefully with our Christian and Muslim neighbors and welcome visitors from around the world. We have synagogues and schools and celebrate Shabbat, just as Jews do all around the world. *Miryam's Dance* is a fictional story, but it is based on our real community.

In Uganda, our Friday night Shabbat services include Hebrew and Luganda songs sung to an African rhythm, accompanied by drums and guitars.

The *toomba* sounds that Miryam hears hints at the beat of a popular Abayudaya version of the song "Hinei Mah Tov/How good it is for us all to be together," which we enjoy singing together with other families.

Our Shabbat dinner often includes matoke (mashed plantains), smoked fish in peanut sauce, and fresh challah. Saturdays usually include a community-wide lunch and learning program. Whether we live in Uganda or the United States or anywhere else in the world, we always have opportunities to celebrate and come together and be joyful.

Your friend,

Rabbi Gershom Sizomu

Learn Luganda!

Abayudaya—translated as "People of Judah" in the Luganda language

kob—Ugandan antelope

maama wange—mother, in Luganda

matoke - a dish made of cooked plantains

Mount Stanley—the highest mountain in Uganda

pawpaw—a large fruit similar in flavor to banana, mango, and pineapple

taata wange—father, in Luganda

Miryam's Favorite Shabbat Food

**Matoke is a traditional dish in Uganda,
made from cooked and mashed plantains.**

- Peel green plantains (or green bananas), and cut them into two-inch pieces.

- Put plantains/bananas in a saucepan, and add water to fill no more than one-quarter of the pot.

- Cover the pot with a lid or banana leaves.

- Steam the plantains/bananas for at least an hour, keeping fire low to allow for simmering.

- Mash the mixture when soft.

- Simmer until ready for serving.

- Serve the matoke on its own or with chicken/fish/bean stew.